An I Can Read Book®

BINGO,
The Best Dog
in the World

by Catherine Siracusa
pictures by Sidney Levitt

HarperCollins*Publishers*

*The illustrations for this book were done
in pen and ink and Winsor & Newton watercolors
on D'Arches watercolor paper.*

I Can Read Book is a registered trademark
of HarperCollins Publishers.

BINGO, THE BEST DOG IN THE WORLD
Text copyright © 1991 by Catherine Siracusa
Illustrations copyright © 1991 by Sidney Levitt
Printed in the U.S.A. All rights reserved.
1   2   3   4   5   6   7   8   9   10
First Edition

Library of Congress Cataloging-in-Publication Data
Siracusa, Catherine.
  Bingo, the best dog in the world / story by Catherine Siracusa ;
pictures by Sidney Levitt.
      p.   cm. — (An I can read book)
  Summary: Sam and her brother Stuart take Bingo to the school dog
show.
    ISBN 0-06-025812-8. — ISBN 0-06-025813-6 (lib. bdg.)
    [1. Dogs—Fiction.   2. Brothers and sisters—Fiction.   3. Dog
shows—Fiction.]   I. Levitt, Sidney, ill.   II. Title.   III. Series.
PZ7.S6215Bi   1991   90-4400
[E]—dc20   CIP
                                                               AC

To Aunt Virginia and Aunt Eva
—C.S.

To Sally Doherty
—S.L.

CONTENTS

1
Bingo's Bath

It was Saturday morning.

Sam and her little brother, Stuart,

sat on the back porch.

"Today is the dog show.

We must give Bingo a bath,"

said Sam.

"Bingo hates baths," said Stuart.

"You will never catch her."

"Yes, I will," said Sam.

"Watch me!"

7

Sam walked slowly toward Bingo.

"Come here, Bingo!" said Sam.

Bingo sat still.

Sam tried to grab Bingo.

Bingo ran!

Stuart laughed.

"Stop laughing!" said Sam.

"Don't you want Bingo to win?"

Sam and Stuart chased Bingo

around and around the yard,

10

but they could not catch her.

11

"Bingo does not want a bath,"
said Stuart.

"Yes, she does," said Sam.

"Bingo loves baths."

"I have an idea," said Sam,

and she ran into the house.

13

Sam came back outside

with some dog treats.

"What are you doing?" asked Stuart.

14

"I am making a line of dog treats

from the yard to the back door,"

said Sam.

"Bingo will eat her way

to the door.

Then we can grab her."

15

Sam and Stuart hid.

"Now what?" said Stuart.

"Shhh!" said Sam. "Just wait."

Bingo looked at the long line

of dog treats.

She walked to the first one

and gobbled it up.

Then she ate the next one

and the next one!

Soon she was on the porch.

Sam and Stuart jumped out.

"We got her!" shouted Stuart.

17

Sam pulled Bingo into the house.

"Come on, Bingo," said Sam.

"Don't you want to win?"

Sam and Stuart

pushed and pulled Bingo

up the stairs and into the bathroom.

"Time for your bubble bath, Bingo,"

said Sam.

"Bingo does not like bubbles,"

said Stuart.

"Yes, she does," said Sam.

"Bingo loves bubble baths."

19

Bingo watched the bubbles.

"Woof! Woof!" she barked.

"Let's get Bingo into the tub,"
said Sam.

"That will not be easy,"
said Stuart.

"We will have to lift her,"
said Sam.

"I will lift her front.
You lift her back."

"I can't hold her!" yelled Stuart.

"I can't hold her either!"

yelled Sam.

Suddenly Bingo jumped—

right into the tub!

"Good dog!" said Sam.

Sam and Stuart washed Bingo.

Then Bingo jumped

out of the bathtub

and shook.

"Stop it, Bingo!" yelled Sam.

"I am all wet!" cried Stuart.

There was a knock on the door.

"Samantha! Stuart!"

"Uh-oh!" said Stuart. "It's Mom!"

"What is going on in there?"

asked Mom.

"We gave Bingo a bath,"

said Sam.

"This bathroom is a mess!"

said Mom.

"I want you to clean it up now!"

"What about the dog show?"

said Stuart.

"We will be late!" said Sam.

"Clean up the bathroom,"

said Mom,

"and I will get Bingo ready.

We will not be late."

Sam and Stuart cleaned up
and went downstairs.
"Bingo looks great,"
said Sam. "Thanks, Mom."

"Can we go now?" said Stuart.

"We will be late!"

"Just a minute," said Sam.

She tied a bright red scarf

around Bingo's neck.

"Now we are ready to go,"

said Sam.

2

On the Way

Sam hugged Bingo.

"I just know you will win!"

she said.

"Bingo looks tired," said Stuart.

"No, Stuart," said Sam,

"Bingo is excited."

"I think she went to sleep,"

said Stuart.

"No," said Sam,

"she is just resting."

Suddenly the car

made an awful noise.

Kazonka! Kazonka!

"What is that?"

said Mom.

The engine made another noise.

32

Kazonka! Kaboing!

Then the car stopped.

"Oh no!" said Sam.

"We will never get

to the dog show on time,"

said Stuart.

"Don't worry," said Mom.

"Maybe I can fix it."

"Mom does not know anything about cars," said Stuart.

"What are we going to do?"

said Sam.

"We will never get

to the dog show now."

Just then a police car stopped.

"Can I help you?"

asked the policeman.

"My car broke down,"

said Mom.

"And we will be late

for the dog show!" said Sam.

The policeman looked at Bingo.

"My dog looks just like your dog,"

he said.

He took some pictures

out of his wallet.

"See, your dog and Vincent

look exactly alike!"

said the policeman.

"Has Vincent ever been

in a dog show?" asked Stuart.

"Vincent won first prize

in the police dog show,"

said the policeman.

"Mom, we have to get Bingo

to *our* dog show!" said Sam.

"Don't worry,"

said the policeman.

"I can get you there

in a hurry."

They all got into the police car.

The policeman

turned on his siren.

"Here we go!" he said.

"Wow!" said Stuart.

Bingo put her head

out the window.

"Vincent does that too,"

said the policeman.

The police car arrived
just in time for the dog show.
"Good luck,"
said the policeman.
"I hope Bingo wins
first prize."

"Good-bye!" said Sam and Stuart.

"Thank you for the ride,"

said Mom.

3

The Dog Show

"Look! There's Hilary and Rover,"
said Sam.

"Hi, Sam! Hi, Bingo!"
yelled Sam's best friend, Hilary.

"What happened?" she asked.

"Our car broke down," said Sam.

"We got to ride in the police car,"
said Stuart.

"It was fun."

"We have to hurry," said Hilary.

"It's time to sign up our dogs."

Bingo yawned

and lay down on the grass.

"Bingo! Wake up!" said Sam.

Bingo did not move.

"Bingo, please!" said Sam.

"Wake up!"

"There are too many dogs here,"

said Stuart.

"Bingo will never win."

"Don't say that!" said Sam.

"I know Bingo will win."

"What is wrong with Bingo?"
asked Hilary.

"Sam fed Bingo
too many dog treats,"
said Stuart.

"Wake up, Bingo!" said Sam.

"I am going to get a hot dog,"
said Stuart. "See you later!"

"Attention please!"

said Mrs. Taylor, the principal.

"Welcome to our first dog show.

We have lots of blue ribbons

and lots of ways to win them.

Let's begin!"

All the dogs were very excited,

except Bingo.

Some dogs did tricks.

Some dogs could shake hands.

Rover could roll over

and play dead.

Bingo yawned.

"I hope they have a blue ribbon

for sleepiest dog," said Sam.

"It's your turn now," said Hilary.

"Get up, Bingo!" said Sam.

Bingo did not move.

"Bingo can do lots of tricks,"

said Sam to Mrs. Taylor.

"Up, Bingo!"

Bingo lay still.

"Attention, please!" said Mrs. Taylor.

"Walk your dogs

in a big circle," she said.

Stuart waved his hot dog in the air.

"Go, Bingo!" he yelled.

Rover saw Stuart's hot dog

and grabbed it.

"No, Rover! No!" shouted Stuart.

"That is my hot dog!"

"Stop, Rover!" cried Hilary.

But Rover would not stop.

He ran to the refreshment table

and jumped.

Crash!

There were hot dogs and buns

and mustard and relish

and paper cups and lemonade

everywhere!

All the dogs started eating,

except Bingo.

Bingo yawned.

Soon the hot dogs were gone.

"Next time our dog show

will be open to all dogs

except hot dogs!"

said Mrs. Taylor.

"I think there is only one dog
who deserves a blue ribbon,"
she said.
"And that dog is Bingo."

Everyone cheered.

Bingo jumped and barked.

"Woof! Woof!"

"*Now* she is awake!" said Stuart.

"Oh, Bingo," said Sam.

"I knew you would win!"

"You are the best dog in the world!"